Russia
the land

Greg Nickles

A Bobbie Kalman Book

The Lands, Peoples, and Cultures Series

 Crabtree Publishing Company
www.crabtreebooks.com

The Lands, Peoples, and Cultures Series
Created by Bobbie Kalman

Project development, editing, and design
First Folio Resource Group, Inc.
  Pauline Beggs
  Tom Dart
  Bruce Krever
  Kathryn Lane
  Debbie Smith

Consultants
Theodore H. Friedgut; Larissa Kisseleva-van Amsterdam; Bella Kotik-Friedgut; Evgueni Petrusevich, Consulate General, Russian Federation, Montreal; Sergei Ulianitsky; and Paul van Amsterdam

Revisions and Updates
Plan B Book Packagers
Redbud Editorial

Coordinating editor
Ellen Rodger

Proofreader
Adrianna Morganelli

Photographs
B. & C. Alexander/Photo Researchers: p. 28 (top); APA/Archive Photos: p. 30; Peter Arkell/Impact: p. 21 (bottom); Cloki/Shutterstock Inc.: cover; CNP/Archive Photos: p. 31 (top); Corbis: p. 30 (top); Corbis/Hulton-Deutsch Collection: p. 6 (bottom); Corbis/Wolfgang Kaehler: p. 29 (bottom); Corbis/Yevgeny Khaldei: p. 7 (bottom); Corbis/Bob Krist: p. 19 (bottom); Corbis/Galen Rowell: p. 17 (top); Corbis/Gregor Schmid: p. 23 (top right); Corbis/Michael T. Sedam: p. 3; Sergiy Dontsov/Shutterstock Inc.: p. 1; Georg Gerster, The National Audubon Society Collection/Photo Researchers: p. 10 (top); Philip Gordon/Impact: p. 25 (top); Jeff Greenberg/Photo Researchers: p. 26 (bottom); Mark Henley/Impact: p. 4; Andy Johnstone/Impact: p. 12 (top), p. 20 (bottom); Wolfgang Kaehler: p. 5, p. 6 (top), p. 10 (bottom), p. 11 (top), p. 13 (top), p. 21 (top left), p. 22 (both), p. 23 (bottom), p. 24, p. 25 (bottom), p. 27 (top); David Kampfner/Impact: p. 29 (bottom); John Kaprielian, The National Audubon Society Collection/Photo Researchers: p. 15 (top); Paolo Koch/Photo Researchers: p. 16 (bottom); Tom & Pat Leeson, The National Audubon Society Collection/Photo Researchers: p. 15 (bottom); Tom McHugh, The National Audubon Society Collection/Photo Researchers: p. 14 (top), p. 17 (bottom); C. Monteath/Hedgehog House/Explorer/Photo Researchers: p. 13 (bottom); Losevsky Pavel/Shutterstock Inc.: p. 7 (top), p. 12 (bottom), p. 19 (top), p. 28 (bottom); Caroline Penn/Impact: p. 20 (top), p. 21 (top right); Jonathan Pile/Impact: p. 18 (top); Reuters/Peter Andrews/Archive Photos: p. 27 (bottom); C. Sappa/Hoa-Qui/Photo Researchers: p. 18 (bottom); Marek Slusarczyk/Shutterstock Inc.: p. 23 (top); Bruce Stephens/Impact: p. 28 (bottom); Roger Tidman, The National Audubon Society Collection/Photo Researchers: p. 14 (bottom); Medvedev Vladimir/Shutterstock Inc.: p. 11 (top); Janet Wishnetsky/Impact: p. 26 (top); Sarah Worker/Impact: p. 9

Map
Jim Chernishenko

Illustrations
David Wysotski, Allure Illustrations: back cover

Cover: The candy colored onion domes of Moscow's St. Basil Cathedral are illuminated at night. The cathedral was built in Red Square between 1555 and 1561.

Title page: A train winds its way through the snow-covered Carpathian mountains.

Icon: *Troikas*, sleighs pulled by three horses, appear at the head of each section.

Back cover: The Kamchatka brown bear is a symbol of Russia.

Library and Archives Canada Cataloguing in Publication

Nickles, Greg, 1969-
        Russia : the land / Greg Nickles. -- 2nd ed., rev.

(Lands, peoples, and cultures series)
Includes index.
ISBN 978-0-7787-9302-1 (bound).--ISBN 978-0-7787-9670-1 (pbk.)

        1. Russia (Federation)--Description and travel--Juvenile literature.
I. Title. II. Series.

DK510.23.N52 2008   j947   C2007-907637-8

Library of Congress Cataloging-in-Publication Data

Nickles, Greg, 1969-
   Russia. The land / Greg Nickles. -- 2nd ed., rev.
      p. cm. -- (Lands, peoples, and cultures series)
   "A Bobbie Kalman Book."
   Includes index.
   ISBN-13: 978-0-7787-9302-1 (rlb)
   ISBN-10: 0-7787-9302-8 (rlb)
   ISBN-13: 978-0-7787-9670-1 (pb)
   ISBN-10: 0-7787-9670-1 (pb)
   1. Russia (Federation)--Juvenile literature. I. Title. II. Series.
   DK510.23.N53 2008
   947--dc22
                                        2007051341

Crabtree Publishing Company
www.crabtreebooks.com   1-800-387-7650

Published in Canada
Crabtree Publishing
616 Welland Ave.
St. Catharines, ON
L2M 5V6

Published in the United States
Crabtree Publishing
PMB16A
350 Fifth Ave., Suite 3308
New York, NY 10118

Published in the United Kingdom
Crabtree Publishing
White Cross Mills
High Town, Lancaster
LA1 4XS

Published in Australia
Crabtree Publishing
386 Mt. Alexander Rd.
Ascot Vale (Melbourne)
VIC 3032

Contents

The Russian Federation, more commonly known as Russia, is the world's largest country. This vast, wintry land is filled with the old and new. Russia's history goes back over a thousand years. The country, however, has existed in its present form only since 1991.

Russia has gone through great changes in the past 20 years and many Russians have struggled with the changes. The country's large mineral and energy resources have pushed growth. In the wilderness, new communities have been built. In the cities, new high rise office towers stand near old churches with onion-shaped domes.

Facts at a glance

Official name: Russian Federation
Capital city: Moscow
Population: 144 million
Land area: 17,075,400 square kilometers
(6,592,850 square miles)
Official language: Russian
Main religion: Russian Orthodox Christianity
Currency: Ruble
National holiday: Independence Day (June 12)

(above) Lake Baikal freezes over during the long, frigid Siberian winters.

(opposite) Rugged hills rise above winding rivers in Kamchatka Peninsula.

Czars and Soviets

Russia's geographic shape and its government have changed many times throughout the centuries. Its most dramatic changes have happened in the last 100 years. During this time, Russians have made great advancements in industry, science, and the arts. They have also suffered through **revolutions**, wars, starvation, and serious **economic** problems.

The Palace in Petrodvorets, near St. Petersburg. The czars used this palace as a summer home.

Ordinary people, including many women, took part in the 1917 revolution.

The time of the czars

For 500 years, Russia was a powerful **empire** governed by rulers called **czars**. The czars lived in luxury, but the lives of the Russian people were miserable. Their anger eventually erupted into a violent revolution that forced the czars from power in 1917. This revolution was led by **socialists**, who took over the country. They believed that the government should own and manage all the country's farms, industries, businesses, and banks. The revolution led to a civil war in which brought suffering and death to millions of Russians.

The Soviet Union

By 1922, Russia gradually reconquered fourteen territories in Europe and Asia that were once part of the Russian Empire. These lands belonged to different **ethnic groups**. Each ethnic group shared a common language, religion, and history. Together with Russia, the fourteen territories formed the Union of **Soviet** Socialist Republics (U.S.S.R.), or Soviet Union, and became a **Communist** state. The U.S.S.R became an industrial and military superpower.

(above) Today, Moscow's Red Square is still a meeting place, but for more democratic purposes.

(left) Over many decades, the Communist government changed Russia from a farming country into an industrial nation with huge government-owned factories.

End of the Soviet Union

In the 1980s, the Soviet Union began to experience severe problems. Some people were unhappy with the limits the Communist government placed on their freedoms. They were also frustrated because the government-run farms and factories were outdated and could not make enough food, clothing, and affordable household goods. When the Communists could not agree with one another about what changes were necessary, the Communist Party fell apart and lost power. Russia and the fourteen other **republics** that made up the Soviet Union split apart to form their own countries. Once the Soviet Union ceased to exist, Russia began to move toward **democracy**. People could finally elect their own representatives to government, and they began to enjoy new freedoms.

Russia is enormous! It stretches half-way around the globe, sits across two continents, and spans eleven time zones. Before people in the far west even get out of bed, those in the far east have finished their day.

Land and water

Russia's landscape is filled with sweeping grasslands, broad valleys, mountains, forests, and **tundra**, which is frozen land where no trees grow. Russia is also a country of water. About 200,000 lakes and thousands of rivers link Russia to major seas and oceans.

Russia has thousands of miles of coastline.

Quick facts on Russia

- The Kaliningrad Territory along the Baltic Sea is part of Russia, although it is not connected to the main part of the country.

- In the far east, Russia sits just 5.4 kilometers (3.4 miles) from Alaska and 4 kilometers (2.5 miles) from Japan.

- Russia belongs to the Commonwealth of Independent States (C.I.S.). The C.I.S. is made up of eleven countries that belonged to the Soviet Union. Besides Russia, these countries are Ukraine, Belarus, Moldova, Georgia, Armenia, Azerbaijan, Kazakhstan, Uzbekistan, Kirghizstan, and Tadzhikistan.

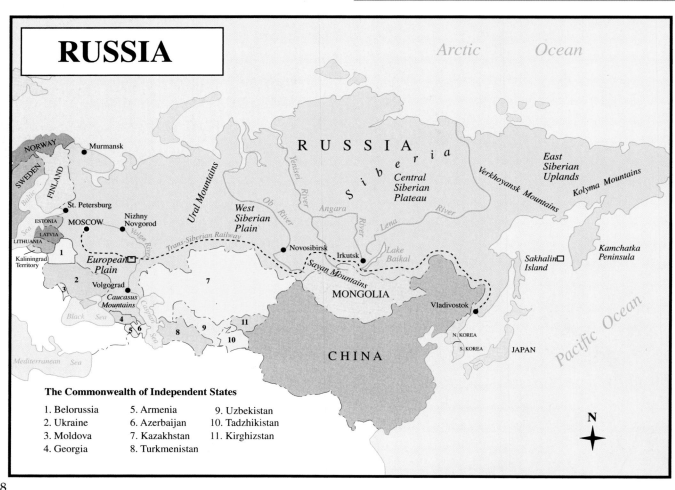

RUSSIA

The Commonwealth of Independent States

1. Belorussia
2. Ukraine
3. Moldova
4. Georgia
5. Armenia
6. Azerbaijan
7. Kazakhstan
8. Turkmenistan
9. Uzbekistan
10. Tadzhikistan
11. Kirghizstan

Russia's landmass occupies much of Europe and and northern Asia. It runs from the Pacific Ocean in the east to the Baltic Sea in the west, and from the Amur river in the south to the Arctic Ocean in the north. Russia landscapes are incredibly diverse. The five main land regions of Russia, from west to east, are the European Plain, the Ural Mountains, the West Siberian Plain, the Central Siberian Plateau, and the East Siberian Uplands.

The European Plain

The European Plain is mostly flat and gently rolling land covered by grass and forests. It is home to Russia's largest cities, Moscow and St. Petersburg. The majority of the population, industries, and farmland are found in this region, as is the Volga River, the longest river in Europe.

The Caucasus Mountains lie south of the European Plain.

9

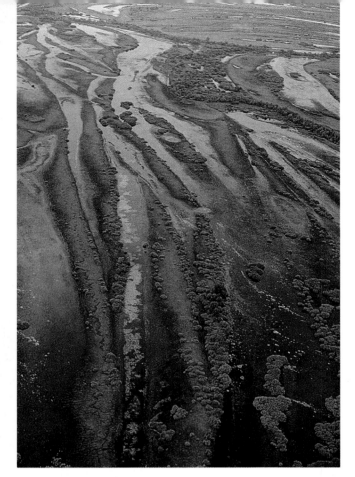

The Ural Mountains

The Ural Mountain chain divides the continents of Europe and Asia. It also marks the border between the western part of Russia and the eastern part, called Siberia. The Urals are extremely rich in metals and minerals. Many industries based on mining have developed in cities throughout the mountains.

Siberian plains and plateaus

The West Siberian Plain is an enormous, flat region covered with endless forests and grassland. This plain, which is the largest area of flat land in the world, also has some of the world's biggest bogs.

The Central Siberian Plateau is a thickly forested region of extremely hot and cold temperatures. Countless streams wind through this area. In the far south, nestled among the peaks of the Sayan and Baikal Mountains, sits Lake Baikal, the largest freshwater lake in the world.

(above) The Ob River floods the West Siberian Plain.

(below) Fields surround a farming village in the rolling Urals.

The East Siberian Uplands

The East Siberian Uplands is an area with mountain ranges such as the Kolyma and Verkhoyansk Mountains. Some ranges jut into the Pacific Ocean, forming **peninsulas**, or narrow pieces of land that project far into the water. The most impressive peninsula is the large Kamchatka, nicknamed "the land of fire and ice." Mostly frozen and covered with snow, Kamchatka also has hot springs and geysers, which gush near-boiling water high into the air.

(right) The Koryak Volcano is one of over 180 volcanoes that crowd Kamchatka Peninsula.

(below) Akkem Lake in Siberia is fed by a mountain glacier and is surrounded by mountains.

Russia is home to over 130 different ethnic groups. Its population is spread unevenly across the country. Three quarters of the people live in the west, while the rest are scattered across Siberia.

Slavic peoples

Most Russians are ethnic Russians, descended from an ancient people called the East Slavs. The East Slavs founded the first Russian land, Kievan Rus, in the ninth century. Ethnic Russians have always played a major role in their country's politics and history. They have also had more **privileges** than other ethnic groups. Most ethnic Russians belong to the Russian Orthodox Church. Russian Orthodoxy is a **denomination** of Christianity, the religion based on the teachings of Jesus Christ, who Christians believe is the son of God.

Two other peoples are descended from the East Slavs — the Ukrainians and Belorussians. Most of these peoples live in the neighboring countries of Ukraine and Belorussia, but millions also live within Russia's borders. Their languages are similar to that of the ethnic Russians, and most follow the Christian religion.

(above) Russians dressed in warm fur coats and hats meet in a Moscow park.

(left) A Russian family shops in a new western-style shopping mall.

Turkic peoples

After the East Slavs, the next largest group in Russia is the Turkic peoples. They include Tatars, Chuvash, Bashkir, Sakhas, and Tuvans. These groups speak different Turkic languages. Most Turkic peoples are Muslim. Their religion, Islam, is based on the teachings of the **prophet** Muhammad. Some Turkic peoples follow other religions. For example, the Chuvash are Christians.

Other groups

Among the many other ethnic groups living in Russia are people who are originally from neighboring countries such as Germany, Poland, Lithuania, Latvia, and Estonia. Hundreds of thousands of Jews also live in Russia, but their numbers are dwindling as many **emigrate** to Israel and other countries. The frozen regions in Siberia's far north and east are thinly populated, but a few peoples, including the Inuit, Aleuts, Chukchi, and Evenki, live there.

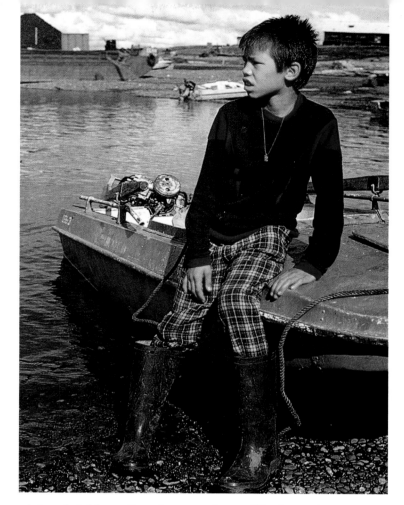

(above) A Nenets boy, from northwest Siberia, waits to go fishing with his father. The Nenets people have traditionally been fishers and reindeer herders.

(below) Russian grandmothers, or babushkas, *read and chat outdoors in northeast Siberia.*

Three main zones of vegetation, or plant life, stretch across Russia. Each zone has its own type of wildlife. From south to north, these zones are the **steppes**, forests, and tundra.

(above) When this bear cub is an adult, it will weigh more than 1,000 times its birth weight.

(below) The musk ox's long, thick fur protects it from Siberia's blizzards and howling winds.

Steppes and forests

Most of Russia's southern regions are steppes, or grasslands, where animals such as antelope, foxes, and gray partridges live. North of the steppes, and far up the sides of many mountains, lie Russia's immense forests. The majority of Russia's forests are **taiga** — dense, swampy woodlands with spruce, pine, and other conifers, or cone-bearing trees. Russia's forests are home to many mammals, including huge populations of deer, elk, beavers, wolves, and the country's best-known animal, the brown bear.

The Russian bear

Brown bears have sharp hearing, excellent eyesight, and a strong sense of smell. They have huge appetites, and eat whatever they find, whether meat or vegetable. During Russia's long, barren winters, brown bears nestle in their dens and fall into a hibernation-like sleep that conserves their energy until spring. Unlike animals that truly hibernate, brown bears can wake up in just minutes if they are in danger!

The Siberian tiger

Another famous forest animal, the Siberian tiger, lives in the mountains in Russia's far east. Siberian tigers can survive in even the coldest temperatures and are superb winter hunters. Their hind legs are longer than their front legs, allowing them to easily bound through deep snow. Unfortunately, humans have hunted these animals almost to **extinction**. Only about 300 survive in the wild.

Treeless tundra

Far in the north, along the coast of the Arctic Ocean, lies the tundra. Covering nearly a quarter of Russia, the tundra is so cold that, even in summertime, only the surface of the marshy soil thaws. Beneath the surface is **permafrost,** or ground that remains frozen year-round. Many animals have adapted to life in the harsh tundra, including Arctic foxes, hares, and mouse-like lemmings. One of the largest tundra inhabitants is the reindeer, the only deer species in which both males and females have antlers.

The snowy owl's speckled plumage helps it blend in with the rocks and snow of its habitat.

The Siberian tiger is the world's largest cat, weighing up to 300 kilograms (660 pounds).

15

Lake Baikal, in south-central Russia, is nicknamed the "Blue Eye of Siberia." It is one of the most remarkable places on earth. Reaching depths of up to 1.6 kilometers (1 mile), it holds more water than any other lake in the world. Lake Baikal is not just exceptional for its size. It is well known for its fascinating plants and animals, and for its stunning beauty.

Nowhere else on earth

Plants and animals thrive in and around the pure, clear water of Lake Baikal. About 1,100 types of plants and 1,550 types of animals live here, many of which are not found anywhere else on the planet. To learn about and preserve the lake's unique wildlife, Russian scientists created their own field of study, called "baikalology," named after Lake Baikal.

(right) Baikal seals like to bask in the sun when they are not swimming.

(below) Lake Baikal holds 20 percent of the world's surface freshwater.

The Baikal seal

The lake's only mammal, the nerpa or Baikal seal, is one of the world's smallest seals. It is also one of the few seals that lives in freshwater instead of saltwater. How Baikal seals reached the lake is a mystery. Most scientists believe that Lake Baikal is too far from the ocean for the seals to have swum there or to have crossed over land. In recent years, many Baikal seals have died from an unknown cause, worrying scientists and visitors to the lake.

The golomyanka

More than 50 species of fish live in the lake, including sturgeon, salmon, and whitefish. Many of these fish are caught by the local people for food. One of the lake's most interesting fish is the golomyanka. The golomyanka lives between 1 to 1.5 kilometers (0.6 to 0.9 miles) below the surface during the day. At night, it swims to the top of the water to dine on tiny creatures called plankton. The golomyanka's transparent body is made largely of fat. If it is still at the surface when the sun comes out, the sun's warmth will cause the fat to melt and the golomyanka's body will turn into an oily blob.

Holy Baikal

People have been drawn to Lake Baikal for centuries because of its beauty. In the past, pilgrims, or travelers on journeys to holy sites, visited the lake because they believed it was filled with powerful spirits. Today, Lake Baikal continues to attract pilgrims, as well as tourists who come to relax at a local resort.

(right) For almost 40 years, scientists and local residents have been protesting the expansion of a pulp plant close to Lake Baikal's shore.

Protecting a treasure

To protect Lake Baikal and its wildlife, the Russian government has passed tough laws restricting development and pollution around the lake. Scientists fear that any pollution, no matter how small the amount, may threaten the purity of the lake's waters and harm its delicate wildlife.

A land of winter

Russia is one of the coldest places in the world. Its long, snowy winters are a time of frigid winds, called *purgas*, and blizzards, or *burans*. For at least six months each year, people must dress in heavy boots, bulky coats, furry hats, and thick gloves. Many Russians love winter, despite the snow and ice. Even in cold weather, they enjoy a brisk walk, stopping outdoors for coffee or ice cream!

Russia's freezing winter temperatures are caused in part by its northerly location. As well, mountains in the west, east, and south block almost all the warm air that blows from the Atlantic, Indian, and Pacific oceans. Instead, very cold, dry air blows from the Arctic Ocean.

(right) A fur hat with ear flaps, called a shapka, *keeps this girl warm in even the coldest weather.*

(top) During the long winters, much of interior Siberia seems endlessly flat and white.

18

Winter's grip

In the heart of winter, many parts of the country look very peaceful and beautiful, covered with icicles and a sparkling blanket of snow. Rivers and lakes freeze over with a thick layer of ice. Some places, especially in northeast Siberia, have temperatures as low as −71°C (−96°F). Skin exposed to these temperatures can freeze within minutes, so people in these areas spend most of their time indoors.

Suddenly summer

Russia is sometimes described as having only two seasons, winter and summer, because spring and autumn are so short. No other country experiences such an extreme range of temperatures. Compared to the deadly lows of winter, summer temperatures can rise as high as 38°C (100°F).

A young girl walks her dog in a forest. The dog wears a sweater to protect it from the cold.

On a warm summer day, sunbathers crowd a beach on the Neva River in St. Petersburg.

Russia's cities are very different from one another. Older cities are filled with beautiful buildings constructed centuries ago. Other cities, especially in Siberia, are younger, steel-and-cement industrial centers. Russia's two largest cities, Moscow and St. Petersburg, have changed since Soviet times. Streets formerly lined with plain, government-run businesses are now alive with street vendors, Western-style stores and restaurants, and colorful billboards. Unfortunately, there are also more homeless people and more crime.

Magnificent Moscow

Moscow is Russia's largest city. It is the country's **capital**, and the center of business, culture, and the Russian Orthodox Church. Thousands of people move to Moscow each year to look for work, making it very crowded. Most of the city's ten million citizens, called Muscovites, live in row upon row of concrete apartment buildings built by the government after World War II ended in 1945.

(above) Most of Moscow's apartments are cramped, so many tenants convert their balconies into extra rooms.

(below) A mother reads as her child naps in one of Moscow's many parks.

Heart of the capital

Moscow's history goes back over 850 years to the time when settlers built a kreml, or fortress, on the banks of the Moskva River. Today, this structure, called the Kremlin, is the heart of the city. Inside the Kremlin are old and beautiful churches, gardens, and some of Russia's government buildings. Outside is Red Square, a favorite place for large gatherings and national parades.

(above) McDonald's opened its first restaurant in the Soviet Union in 1990.

(below) Guards march through Red Square past Lenin's tomb. The preserved body of the first leader of the Communist Party has been on display since 1930 and still attracts visitors.

(above) Buildings and churches crowd the streets of downtown Moscow.

21

Stunning St. Petersburg

St. Petersburg was founded in 1703 by Czar
Peter the Great. He built the city as a symbol of
the Russian empire's power and beauty.
St. Petersburg, which was also known as
Petrograd and Leningrad in the 1900s, served as
the country's capital from 1712 to 1918. The city
is filled with stunning palaces, sculptures, and
fountains. St. Petersburg is also a well known
center for ballet, music, and literature.

White nights

St. Petersburg is located in the far north where,
for three weeks each June, it is light for almost
24 hours of the day. The sun sets at 2 a.m. and
rises at 2:30 a.m, with only a half hour of
twilight in between. These "White Nights" are
celebrated with festivals of music and dancing.

*Catherine the Great's palace in St. Petersburg, reflects
the Czaritza's lavish taste.*

*Water is everywhere in St. Petersburg. The city was
built on a hundred islands in the Neva River delta.*

(above) **In the city of Nizhny Novgorod, a Russian Orthodox cathedral sits next to loading docks on the Volga River.**

(below) **Vladivostok is a major naval base on the Pacific Coast.**

A transport truck is loaded with lumber at a port on Sakhalin Island, off Russia's southeastern coast.

Since the early 1990s, Russia's post-Communist government has been making major changes to the economy. Instead of owning all of Russia's industries and controlling the prices of all goods, the government transferred control and ownership of its farms, factories, businesses, and banks to private businesses that compete with one another for customers.

Rich and poor

Russia now has several billionaires, who grew wealthy after the introduction of a **free-market** economy. Most of these new billionaires own banks, manufacturing companies, and oil, gas, and mineral exploration and development companies. They have built lavish homes, mostly in Moscow. Russia also has many people who have not economically benefitted from changes to the country's economy. They mostly live in rural areas where jobs are hard to come by.

Russia went through a difficult period of economic change in the 1990s as the country stuggled to adjust to a **capitalist** economic system. Millions of people lost their jobs and had to adjust to a new way of life. Without government controls on prices, the cost of food increased so much that some people could barely afford to eat and pensioners had a hard time making ends meet. Since that time, things have improved. Russia's vast reserves of oil and gas have helped the economy grow and stabilize. Russia now has a growing, well-educated **middle class**.

New business

Thousands of Russians started new businesses over the last decade, something that was illegal during the Soviet era. Wealthy Russians have invested in large businesses such as factories, mines, and oil companies. Most new businesses, however, are small. They include restaurants, hair salons, and sidewalk stalls, where people of all ages sell magazines, homemade crafts, and fruit and vegetables that they grow in their gardens in the countryside.

Abundant resources

Russia's natural resources lie mostly untapped in hard-to-reach parts of Siberia. They include vast forests and huge deposits of minerals such as gold, diamonds, iron ore, copper, nickel, and lead. The country also has large **reserves** of coal, natural gas, and oil. Much of the equipment used to **extract** these resources is old-fashioned, wasteful, and sometimes dangerous. To modernize these industries, Russia has developed partnerships with foreign companies that specialize in forestry, mining, and energy.

(top) Many people work in the manufacturing industry, making useful, everyday products such as boots.

(below) A fur coat stall in an outdoor market is very popular with people preparing for winter! Market stalls like these help fuel the economy.

Russia has enormous areas of rich farmland. Its long coasts and rivers link it to some of the world's largest stocks of seafood. Like all other parts of the economy, Russia's farming and fishing industries have been changing to the free-market system. The government still owns some Russian farms, but it is trying to encourage farmers to buy them as private businesses. Some **entrepreneurs** have even started agribusiness companies to **process** and sell the products grown on Russian farms.

Fertile farmland

Russia is one of the world's top producers of grains such as wheat and barley. These crops, which thrive in Russia's short, dry summer, grow mainly in the steppes. In the lush Caucasus Mountains, farmers plant cherries, apricots, melons, and other fruits and vegetables. In Siberia, where the growing season is too short for crops, families often grow fruit and vegetables in greenhouses. Throughout the country, farmers raise cattle, pigs, chickens, and other livestock for meat, eggs, and milk.

So much food!

One of the greatest challenges farmers hope to solve is waste. Russia's farms produce huge amounts of food, but much spoils before it gets to market because there is no efficient system to store, transport, and package it.

(left) A tractor adds to a huge pile of harvested beets.

(top) Herders milk goats in the Caucasus Mountains.

Fishing fleets

Large Russian fishing fleets sail the country's rivers, lakes, and oceans. They haul in vast catches of seafood, including salmon, haddock, cod, and herring. Many of the country's largest ships are like floating factories. Fishers can clean and **process** their catches onboard. Russia's most famous seafood is caviar. This salty delicacy is made from the eggs of the sturgeon fish, caught mainly in the Volga River and Caspian Sea.

The number of fish in Russia and throughout the world has shrunk in recent years due to pollution and overfishing. Smaller fish stocks and increasing competition from other countries' fishing fleets, has meant Russia's fishers have been hauling in smaller and smaller catches.

(above) Many Russian families with small weekend cottages, called dachas, have vegetable gardens where they grow some of their own food.

(below) Fishermen haul in a large catch of salmon. They have had a very successful day!

If you are not in the city, getting from one place to another in Russia can be a challenge! Cities have good public transit services, such as buses, streetcars, and subway trains. In rural areas of the country, people have to travel great distances in difficult weather to reach their destinations.

Russia has few highways, and paved roads are rare outside of cities. Only one of every twenty Russians owns an automobile. Instead, people walk, cycle, or use snowmobiles, trains, and boats to get around. In some rural places, horse-drawn wagons and, very rarely, traditional three-horse sleighs called *troikas* are used for travel. Flying on a plane or helicopter is often the only way to get to the most remote parts of the country.

(above) A cyclist in snowy St. Petersburg waits for a freight train to pass at a railway crossing.

(below) People crowd the escalators in a Moscow subway station during rush hour.

On the water

A network of canals connect Russia's cities to rivers and seas. These water routes are important shipping paths, although some northern rivers are frozen over for several months each year. Major seaports, such as St. Petersburg, Vladivostock, and Murmansk, are kept open as long as possible during the winter by huge, powerful ships that break up the pack ice.

The mighty Trans-Siberian Railway

Many rail systems carry goods and passengers across the western part of Russia. Only one major line crosses the huge expanse of Siberia. The Trans-Siberian Railway runs between Moscow and Vladivostock, on the Pacific coast. At 9.240 kilometers (5,747 miles), it covers about a third of the distance around the planet. It took over fifteen years to construct the line, which was completed in 1905. Many workers died laying the tracks due to terrible accidents, the extreme Siberian climate, and the lack of proper food and water.

All aboard!

Passengers riding the Trans-Siberian spend between seven and ten days on comfortable trains with sleeping compartments and a dining car. Along the way, they pass through seven time zones and make over 90 stops at cities, towns, and remote villages. During a stop, many passengers get off the train to buy tasty homemade meals sold by local women along the train platform. Stops are just a few minutes long, and the train gives just one warning blast before departing. Passengers must get back onboard quickly so they are not left behind!

(top) Some peoples of the Arctic, such as the Nentsy, still travel by reindeer sled.

(below) The Trans-Siberian makes its way across the expanse of south-central Siberia.

(above) Russian cosmonauts take a last look at the departing crew of the Atlantis space shuttle before closing Mir's hatch.

(below) Laika sits in her air-conditioned cabin ready to blast off on Sputnik 2.

Russia became a world leader in space exploration in 1957 when, as part of the Soviet Space Agency, it launched Sputnik 1, the world's first artificial **satellite**. Today, the Russian Federal Space Agency's (RKA) main goals include improving telephone, television, and weather forecasting services with new satellites. The agency is also a partner in the International Space Station (ISS), a space research facility that orbits Earth. The Russian Space Agency suffered from a lack of funding in the years after the fall of Communism. Since the Russian economy has recovered, the Agency has been given more government money. The Agency has also made money through space tourism. For $20 million, space tourists were trained and sent into space for a ten-day stay at the International Space Station.

The Space Race

Space tourism is a far cry from the early days of the Russian space program. The launch of Sputnik 1 stunned the world and was a triumph for Soviet **cosmonauts**, or astronauts. Shortly after, they launched Sputnik 2, which carried the first passenger — a dog named Laika — into space. Although Laika lived only a week, Sputnik 2 was considered another great success. To compete with the Soviets in space exploration, the United States created NASA, the National Aeronautics and Space Administration. Over the next 30 years, the two countries raced to be the first to make important space breakthroughs. This competition was called the Space Race. For decades, the Soviet Union worked to put a permanent space station in orbit. In 1986, it launched Mir, which means "peace." Mir became the longest-running and most successful space station ever.

The Mir space station prepares for a docking with a space shuttle bringing supplies.

During its thirteen-year mission, crew members from Russia and other countries visited the space station. Mir hosted countless science experiments, docked with American space shuttles, and even survived a fire and a crash with a small cargo ship. Scientists on Mir learned valuable lessons about what it is like to live for long periods of time in space.

The International Space Station

Russia is an important member of the team of countries working on the International Space Station. These countries hope that the ISS will continue Mir's mission of studying life on Earth and in space. The RKA transport astronauts, cosmonauts, and space tourists to and from the ISS, and builds laboratory modules.

Space firsts
The Soviets scored many important firsts in space, including:

 the first moon probe (Luna 1, 1959)

 the first human in space and the first human to orbit the earth (Yuri Gagarin, aboard Vostock 1, 1961)

 the first woman in space (Valentina Tereshkova, aboard Vostock 6, 1963)

 the first docking of two crewed spacecrafts and exchange of crews (Soyuz 4 and Soyuz 5, 1969)

 the first experimental space station (Salyut 1, 1971)

 the longest consecutive stay in space (438 days by Valery Polyakov, aboard Mir, 1994)

Glossary

capital A city where the government of a state or country is located

capitalist A supporter of an economic system where wealth is made and owned by individuals and corporations

Communist A person who believes in an economic system where the country's natural resources, businesses, and industries are owned and controlled by the government

cosmonaut A Russian (or Soviet) astronaut

czar The title given to Russian emperors

democracy A form of government in which representatives are elected to make decisions for a society

denomination An organized religious group within a faith

economic The way a country organizes and manages its businesses, industries, and money

emigrate To move to a new country

empire A group of countries or territories having the same ruler

entrepreneur A person who owns their own business

ethnic group A group of people who share a common race, language, heritage, or religion

extinction When a type of animal or species no longer exists

extract To remove something from its natural place, like oil from the earth

free-market Trade without high taxes or strict government control

middle class People who have moderate incomes and are not struggling to survive

peninsula A point of land that juts into a body of water

permafrost Land in cold climates that remains frozen all year long

privilege A special right

process To treat or prepare something by a special method

prophet A person who is believed to speak on behalf of God

republic A country that is not led by a king or queen

reserve A large supply of an item stored for future use

revolution An uprising or war against a government

satellite A man-made object that revolves around the earth or other bodies in space

Socialist A member of a political party that follows an economic system whereby the country's natural resources, businesses, industries, and politics are controlled by the entire community

Soviet Having to do with, or a citizen of, the Union of Soviet Socialist Republics (U.S.S.R.), which existed from 1922 to 1991

steppes A large, treeless plain

taiga Damp, swampy forests

tundra A large plain where little vegetation grows and which remains frozen all year

Index

2